Wilde on Love

Warbler Press

ISBN 978-1-7347353-4-5 (paperback)
ISBN 978-1-7347353-5-2 (e-book)

warblerpress.com

Printed in the United States of America. This edition is printed with chlorine-free ink on acid-free interior paper made from 30% post-consumer waste recycled material.

Warbler Press Contemplations current and forthcoming titles at warblerpress.com

Wilde on Love

Oscar Wilde

EDITED BY ULRICH BAER

CONTENTS

Wilde on Love

All I do know is that life cannot be understood without much charity, cannot be lived without much charity. It is love, and not German philosophy, that is the true explanation of this world, whatever may be the explanation of the next.

I used to think ambition the great thing. It is not. Love is the great thing in the world. There is nothing but love.

When one is in love, one always begins by deceiving one's self, and one always ends by deceiving others. That is what the world calls a romance.

Shallow sorrows and shallow loves live on. The loves and sorrows that are great are destroyed by their own plenitude.

I really don't see anything romantic in proposing. It is very romantic to be in love. But there is nothing romantic about a definite proposal. Why, one may be accepted. One usually is, I believe. Then the excitement is all over. The very essence of romance is uncertainty. If ever I get married, I'll certainly try to forget the fact.

The only way to behave to a woman is to make love to her, if she is pretty, and to some one else, if she is plain.

Robert, men can love what is beneath them—things unworthy, stained, dishonoured. We women worship when we love; and when we lose our worship, we lose everything. Oh! don't kill my love for you, don't kill that!

Children begin by loving their parents; after a time, they judge them; rarely, if ever, do they forgive them.

The world has grown suspicious of anything that looks like a happily married life.

In married life three is company and two none.

If you are not too long, I will wait here for you all my life.

I see when men love women they give them a little of their lives. But women when they love give everything.

SIR ROBERT CHILTERN: There was your mistake. There was your error. The error all women commit. Why can't you women love us, faults and all? Why do you place us on monstrous pedestals? We have all feet of clay, women as well as men; but when we men love women, we love them knowing their weaknesses, their follies, their imperfections, love them all the more, it may be, for that reason. It is not the perfect, but the imperfect, who have need of love. It is when we are wounded by our own hands, or by the hands of others, that love should come to cure us—else what use is love at all? All sins, except a sin against itself, Love should forgive. All lives, save loveless lives, true Love should pardon. A man's love is like that. It is wider, larger, more human than a woman's. Women think that they are making ideals of men. What they are making of us are false idols merely. You made your false idol of me, and I had not the courage to come down, show you my wounds, tell you my weaknesses. I was afraid that I might lose your love, as I have lost it now. And so, last night you ruined my life for me—yes, ruined it! What this woman asked of me was nothing compared to what she offered to me. She offered security, peace, stability. The sin of my youth, that I had thought was buried, rose up in front of me, hideous, horrible, with its hands at my throat. I could have killed it for ever, sent it back into its tomb, destroyed its record, burned the one witness against me. You prevented me. No one but you, you know it. And now what is there before me but public disgrace, ruin, terrible shame, the mockery of the world, a lonely dishonoured life, a lonely dishonoured death, it may be, some day? Let women make no more ideals of men! let them not put them on alters and bow before them, or they may ruin other lives as completely as you—you whom I have so wildly loved—have ruined mine!

Always! That is a dreadful word. It makes me shudder when I hear it.

Women are so fond of using it. They spoil every romance by trying to make it last for ever. It is a meaningless word, too. The only difference between a caprice and a lifelong passion is that the caprice lasts a little longer.

She was a curious woman, whose dresses always looked as if they had been designed in a rage and put on in a tempest. She was usually in love with somebody, and, as her passion was never returned, she had kept all her illusions.

Men marry because they are tired; women, because they are curious: both are disappointed.

To love oneself is the beginning of a lifelong romance.

You know you loved me; and love is a very wonderful thing. I suppose that when a man has once loved a woman, he will do anything for her, except continue to love her?

A woman who can keep a man's love, and love him in return, has done all the world wants of women, or should want of them.

Loveless marriages are horrible. But there is one thing worse than an absolutely loveless marriage. A marriage in which there is love, but on one side only; faith, but on one side only; devotion, but on one side only, and in which of the two hearts one is sure to be broken.

LADY CHILTERN: It is love, Robert. Love, and only love. For both of us a new life is beginning.

.

Between men and women there is no friendship possible. There is passion, enmity, worship, love, but no friendship.

Love—well, not love at first sight, but love at the end of the season, which is so much more satisfactory.

Love is easily killed. Oh! how easily love is killed.

Surely Love is a wonderful thing. It is more precious than emeralds, and dearer than fine opals. Pearls and pomegranates cannot buy it, nor is it set forth in the marketplace. It may not be purchased of the merchants, nor can it be weighed out in the balance for gold.

"Death is a great price to pay for a red rose," cried the Nightingale, "and Life is very dear to all. It is pleasant to sit in the green wood, and to watch the Sun in his chariot of gold, and the Moon in her chariot of pearl. Sweet is the scent of the hawthorn, and sweet are the bluebells that hide in the valley, and the heather that blows on the hill. Yet Love is better than Life, and what is the heart of a bird compared to the heart of a man?"

"Be happy," cried the Nightingale, "be happy; you shall have your red rose. I will build it out of music by moonlight, and stain it with my own heart's-blood. All that I ask of you in return is that you will be a true lover, for Love is wiser than Philosophy, though she is wise, and mightier than Power, though he is mighty. Flame-coloured are his wings, and coloured like flame is his body. His lips are sweet as honey, and his breath is like frankincense."

"What a silly thing Love is," said the Student as he walked away. "It is not half as useful as Logic, for it does not prove anything, and it is always telling one of things that are not going to happen, and making one believe things that are not true. In fact, it is quite unpractical, and, as in this age to be practical is everything, I shall go back to Philosophy and study Metaphysics."

"Any place you love is the world to you," exclaimed a pensive Catherine Wheel, who had been attached to an old deal box in early life, and prided herself on her broken heart; "but love is not fashionable any more, the poets have killed it. They wrote so much about it that nobody believed them, and I am not surprised. True love suffers, and is silent.

I would not a bit mind sleeping in the cool grass in summer, and when winter came on sheltering myself by the warm close-thatched rick, or under the penthouse of a great barn, provided I had love in my heart.

When you really want love you will find it waiting for you.

I remember talking once on this subject to one of the most beautiful personalities I have ever known: a woman, whose sympathy and noble kindness to me, both before and since the tragedy of my imprisonment, have been beyond power and description; one who has really assisted me, though she does not know it, to bear the burden of my troubles more than any one else in the whole world has, and all through the mere fact of her existence, through her being what she is—partly an ideal and partly an influence: a suggestion of what one might become as well as a real help towards becoming it; a soul that renders the common air sweet, and makes what is spiritual seem as simple and natural as sunlight or the sea: one for whom beauty and sorrow walk hand in hand, and have the same message. On the occasion of which I am thinking I recall distinctly how I said to her that there was enough suffering in one narrow London lane to show that God did not love man, and that wherever there was any sorrow, though but that of a child, in some little garden weeping over a fault that it had or had not committed, the whole face of creation was completely marred. I was entirely wrong. She told me so, but I could not believe her. I was not in the sphere in which such belief was to be attained to.

Now it seems to me that love of some kind is the only possible explanation of the extraordinary amount of suffering that there is in the world. I cannot conceive of any other explanation. I am convinced that there is no other, and that if the world has indeed, as I have said, been built of sorrow, it has been built by the hands of love, because in no other way could the soul of man, for whom the world was made, reach the full stature of its perfection. Pleasure for the beautiful body, but pain for the beautiful soul.

Those who are faithful know only the trivial side of love: it is the faithless who know love's tragedies.

"What a fuss people make about fidelity!" exclaimed Lord Henry. "Why, even in love it is purely a question for physiology. It has nothing to do with our own will. Young men want to be faithful, and are not; old men want to be faithless, and cannot: that is all one can say."

"I don't think I am likely to marry, Harry. I am too much in love."

A grande passion is the privilege of people who have nothing to do. That is the one use of the idle classes of a country.

My dear boy, the people who love only once in their lives are really the shallow people. What they call their loyalty, and their fidelity, I call either the lethargy of custom or their lack of imagination. Faithfulness is to the emotional life what consistency is to the life of the intellect—simply a confession of failure. Faithfulness! I must analyse it some day. The passion for property is in it. There are many things that we would throw away if we were not afraid that others might pick them up.

It was the passions about whose origin we deceived ourselves that tyrannized most strongly over us. Our weakest motives were those of whose nature we were conscious. It often happened that when we thought we were experimenting on others we were really experimenting on ourselves.

To be in love is to surpass one's self.

The real drawback to marriage is that it makes one unselfish. And unselfish people are colourless. They lack individuality. Still, there are certain temperaments that marriage makes more complex. They retain their egotism, and add to it many other egos. They are forced to have more than one life. They become more highly organized, and to be highly organized is, 1 should fancy, the object of man's existence.

When poverty creeps in at the door, love flies in through the window.

I wish you would fall in love. Love makes people good, and what you said was wicked.

I cannot understand how any one can wish to shame the thing he loves.

Love is a more wonderful thing than art. They are both simply forms of imitation

There is always something ridiculous about the emotions of people whom one has ceased to love.

Women love us for our defects. If we have enough of them, they will forgive us everything, even our intellects.

A man can be happy with any woman, as long as he does not love her.

"Not with women," said the duchess, shaking her head; "and women rule the world. I assure you we can't bear mediocrities. We women, as some one says, love with our ears, just as you men love with your eyes, if you ever love at all."

Romance lives by repetition, and repetition converts an appetite into an art. Besides, each time that one loves is the only time one has ever loved. Difference of object does not alter singleness of passion. It merely intensifies it. We can have in life but one great experience at best, and the secret of life is to reproduce that experience as often as possible.

Of course, married life is merely a habit, a bad habit. But then one regrets the loss even of one's worst habits. Perhaps one regrets them the most. They are such an essential part of one's personality.

Woman begins by resisting a man's advances and ends by blocking his retreat.

Hatred is blind, as well as love.

I don't think there is a woman in the world who would not be a little flattered if one made love to her. It is that which makes women so irresistibly adorable.

LADY CAROLINE. It's perfectly scandalous the amount of bachelors who are going about society. There should be a law passed to compel them all to marry within twelve months.

LADY STUTFIELD. But if they're in love with some one who, perhaps, is tied to another?

LADY CAROLINE. In that case, Lady Stutfield, they should be married off in a week to some plain respectable girl, in order to teach them not to meddle with other people's property.

MRS. ALLONBY. I don't think that we should ever be spoken of as other people's property. All men are married women's property. That is the only true definition of what married women's property really is. But we don't belong to any one.

MRS. ALLONBY. When Ernest and I were engaged, he swore to me positively on his knees that he had never loved any one before in the whole course of his life. I was very young at the time, so I didn't believe him, I needn't tell you. Unfortunately, however, I made no enquiries of any kind till after I had been actually married four or five months. I found out then that what he had told me was perfectly true. And that sort of thing makes a man so absolutely uninteresting.

Men always want to be a woman's first love. That is their clumsy vanity. We women have a more subtle instinct about things. What we like is to be a man's last romance.

MRS. ALLONBY. Do you know, Lady Caroline, I don't think the frivolity of the wife has ever anything to do with it. More marriages are ruined nowadays by the common sense of the husband than by anything else. How can a woman be expected to be happy with a man who insists on treating her as if she were a perfectly rational being?

LADY HUNSTANTON. My dear!

MRS. ALLONBY. Man, poor, awkward, reliable, necessary man belongs to a sex that has been rational for millions and millions of years. He can't help himself. It is in his race. The History of Woman is very different. We have always been picturesque protests against the mere existence of common sense. We saw its dangers from the first.

LADY STUTFIELD. The Ideal Man, then, in his relations to us.

LADY CAROLINE. He would probably be extremely realistic.

MRS. CAROLINE. The Ideal Man! Oh, the Ideal Man should talk to us as if we were goddesses, and treat us as if we were children. He should refuse all our serious requests, and gratify every one of our whims. He should encourage us to have caprices, and forbid us to have missions. He should always say much more than he means, and always mean much more than he says.

LADY HUNSTANTON. But how could he do both, dear?

MRS. ALLONBY. He should never run down other pretty women. That would show he had no taste, or make one suspect that he had too much. No; he should be nice about them all, but say that somehow they don't attract him.

LADY STUTFIELD. Yes, that is always very, very pleasant to hear about other women.

MRS. ALLONBY. If we ask him a question about

anything, he should give us an answer all about our-selves. He should invariably praise us for whatever qualities he knows we haven't got. But he should be pitiless, quite pitiless, in reproaching us for the vir-tues that we have never dreamed of possessing. He should never believe that we know the use of useful things. That would be unforgiveable. But he should shower on us everything we don't want.

LADY CAROLINE. As far as I can see, he is to do nothing but pay bills and compliments.

MRS. ALLONBY. He should persistently compromise us in public, and treat us with absolute respect when we are alone. And yet he should be always ready to have a perfectly terrible scene, whenever we want one, and to become miserable, absolutely miserable, at a moment's notice, and to overwhelm us with just reproaches in less than twenty minutes, and to be positively violent at the end of half an hour, and to leave us for ever at a quarter to eight, when we have to go and dress for dinner. And when, after that, one has seen him for really the last time, and he has refused to take back the little things he has given one, and promised never to communicate with one again, or to write one any foolish letters, he should be perfectly broken-hearted, and telegraph to one all day long, and send one little notes every half-hour by a private hansom, and dine quite alone at the club, so that every one should know how unhappy he was. And after a whole dreadful week, during which one has gone about everywhere with one's husband, just to show how absolutely lonely one was, he may be given a third last parting, in the evening, and then, if his conduct has been quite irreproachable, and one has behaved really badly to him, he should be allowed to admit that he has been entirely in the wrong, and when he has admitted that, it becomes a woman's duty to forgive, and one can do it all over again from the beginning, with variations.

HESTER. It is right that they should be punished, but don't let them be the only ones to suffer. If a man and woman have sinned, let them both go forth into the desert to love or loathe each other there. Let them both be branded. Set a mark, if you wish, on each, but don't punish the one and let the other go free. Don't have one law for men and another for women. You are unjust to women in England. And till you count what is a shame in a woman to be an infamy in a man, you will always be unjust, and Right, that pillar of fire, and Wrong, that pillar of cloud, will be made dim to your eyes, or be not seen at all, or if seen, not regarded.

Oh! talk to every woman as if you loved her, and to every man as if he bored you, and at the end of your first season you will have the reputation of possessing the most perfect social tact.

LADY HUNSTANTON. How clever you are, my dear! You never mean a single word you say.

LADY STUTFIELD. Thank you, thank you.

One should always be in love. That is the reason one should never marry.

A gentleman is one who never hurts anyone's feelings unintentionally.

Only love can keep any one alive. And boys are care-less often and without thinking give pain, and we always fancy that when they come to man's estate and know us better they will repay us. But it is not so. The world draws them from our side, and they make friends with whom they are happier than they are with us, and have amusements from which we are barred, and interests that are not ours: and they are unjust to us often, for when they find life bitter they blame us for it, and when they find it sweet we do not taste its sweetness with them.

Who, being loved, is poor? Oh, no one.

Women are never disarmed by compliments. Men always are. That is the difference between the sexes.

The one charm about marriage is that it makes a life of deception absolutely necessary for both parties.

Deceiving others. That is what the world calls a romance.

How marriage ruins a man! It is as demoralizing as cigarettes, and far more expensive.

There is nothing in the world like the devotion of a married woman. It is a thing no married man knows anything about.

Yet each man kills the thing he loves
By each let this be heard,
Some do it with a bitter look,
Some with a flattering word,
The coward does it with a kiss,
The brave man with a sword!

Some kill their love when they are young,
And some when they are old;
Some strangle with the hands of Lust,
Some with the hands of Gold:
The kindest use a knife, because
The dead so soon grow cold.

Some love too little, some too long,
Some sell, and others buy;
Some do the deed with many tears,
And some without a sigh:
For each man kills the thing he loves,
Yet each man does not die.

But him whom he could not hold by love, he would not hold by force.

Wilde in Love

(Letters)

Oscar Wilde's correspondence is available as *The Collected Letters of Oscar Wilde*, edited by Merlon Holland and Rupert Hart-Davis (London: Fourth Estate, 2000). The editors adapt Wilde's unbridled use of dashes and stenographic characters to standard English, and otherwise make readable what Wilde had often written in haste and intended only for his recipient's eyes. The letters to Lord Alfred Douglas, nicknamed Bosie by Wilde, were published by William Andrew Clark, Jr., in a private, limited edition, as *Some Letters from Oscar Wilde to Alfred Douglas, 1892-1897* (San Francisco, 1924). The edition includes facsimiles of the letters and a single letter from Bosie addressed to Wilde that is here transcribed, to be best of our knowledge, for the first time.

That edition includes an essay by legendary American bookseller, A. S. W. Rosenbach, who justifies the publication of personal letters, also sanctioned by Wilde's literary executor, his son Vyvyan Holland, as a way to correct the myth Wilde perpetuated about himself in writings published after his release from prison in 1895, and the impression Lord Douglas gave in memoirs and other writings in the 1930s. The letters have been dated according to the timeline established by Holland and Hart-Davis.

Nine copies of the book exist in the United States, in rare book depositories, with an additional three copies held in England, Ireland, and Canada.

Both Wilde and Douglas had something to gain from hiding the truth of their relationship in a series of publications, including Wilde's *De Profundis* and Douglas's memoir and other writings, even if both of them refused, after Wilde's discharge from prison and exile in France, to live a lie. The personal letters included here offer a somewhat different picture. In these letters Wilde does not shield himself with irony and wit. He is exposed to our judgment, as he had been exposed to the cruel judgment of English society and the opprobrium of friends and associates when some of his letters were read publicly in court during his trial.

[? February 1893]

Babbacombe
Babbacombe Cliffs.

MY DEAREST BOSIE

I have written to yr. man, and have received no reply from him—which is most annoying—as things are the wrong colour without gold to light them up—Are you working? I hope so—do get a good crammer—

I am rather unhappy as I can't write—I don't know why—things are all wrong. Have you been writing lovely sonnets? I never got the Spirit-Lamp—not even a cheque—!

My charge for the sonnet is £300. Who on earth *is* the Editor? He must be rented. I hear he is hiding at Salisbury

—with best love
Evyr—
OSCAR

[?12-15 April 1893]

DEAREST BOY—

We have only just finished

<u>Act 2!!</u>

Dont wait

Order, of course, what you want. Lunch, 1.30 tomorrow: at
Albemarle—I do not rehearse tomorrow at all.

Evyr
OSCAR.

❧

[?20 April 1893]

16 Tite Street
S.W.

MY DEAREST BOY,

Life here is much the same—I find a chastened pleasure in
being shaved in Air Street—you are always enquired after—and
sonnet-like allusions made to your gilt silk hair. I saw an emis-
sary from Mansfield, the actor, this morning. I think of writing
'The Cardinal of Avignon' at once—If I had peace, I would do it.
Mansfield would act it splendidly.

Max on Cosmetics in the Yellow Book is wonderful—: enough
style for a large school—and all very precious and thought-out:
quite delightfully wrong and fascinating.

I had a frantic telegram from Edward Shelley, of all people! asking me to see him. When he came he was of course in trouble for money—As he betrayed me grossly I, of course, gave him money and was kind to him. I find that forgiving one's enemies is a most curious morbid pleasure—perhaps I should check it.

With love
Evyr.
OSCAR.

[? May 1893]

16 Tite Street
S.W.

MY DEAR BOY:

No letter from you yet. But I hope to find a line when I go home—I lunched with Prince Troubetzkoi and Mrs. Chanler this afternoon—He has done a lovely picture of her—and would do a beautiful one of you. I talked to him about you. He is going down to the Batterseas to finish his portrait of Cyril but will be back in the autumn. You really must be painted, and also have an ivory statue executed.

Willard, the actor, lunches with me on Thursday to talk business—I hope to lure him to give me some of "the gold the gryphon guards in rude Armenia"

Are you coming up on Wednesday: if so, do dine with me.

Ever yours
OSCAR

Saturday [9 September 1893]

MY DEAR BOSIE

Thanks for your telegram which I got last night on my arrival from Jersey—where I had been for a night, on my way over, to see a performance of my play by Miss Lingard and the South Company—it was rather good, and I had a great reception from a crowded house—The General Arbuthnot was excellent, and very nice—I entertained the actors afterwards at supper—I am off to Goring now—to try and settle up things—I don't know what to do about the place—whether to stay there or not—and the servants are a worry—I went round to see Lane just now, but he is in Paris with Rothenstein—I hope you will get proofs soon—I suppose you are in Devon for your brother's marriage—give him my best wishes.

Evyr.
OSCAR

∾

[circa 20 December 1893]

MY DEAREST BOY

Thanks for your letter—I am overwhelmed by the wings of vulture creditors—and out of sorts—but I am happy in the knowledge that we are friends again—and that our love has passed through the shadow and the night of estrangement and sorrow and come out rose-crowned as of old—let us always be infinitely dear to each other, as indeed we have been always.

I hear Bobbie is in town—lame and bearded! isn't it awful? I have not seen him yet. Lady Thompson has appeared—he is extremely anxious to devotee his entire life to me—Tree has written a long apologetic letter—his reasons are so reasonable that I cannot understand them—a cheque is the only argument I recognize—Hare returns to town early next week. I am going to make an effort to induce him to see that my new play is a masterpiece—but I have grave doubts. This is all the news. How horrid news is! I think of you daily—and am always devotedly

Yours,
OSCAR

[circa 16 April, 1894]

MY DEAREST BOY,

Your telegram has just arrived—it was a joy to get it—but I miss you so much—the gay gilt and gracious lad has gone away—and hate every one else—they are tedious—also I am in the purple valleys of despair—and no gold coins are dropping down from heavens to gladden me—London is very dangerous—'Writters' come out at night and writ one—the roaring of creditors towards dawn is frightful—and solicitors are getting rabies and biting people—

How I envy you under Giotto's Tower, or sitting in the loggia looking at that green and gold god of Cellini's—You must write poems like apple blossoms—

The "Yellow Book" has appeared—it is dull and loathsome: a great failure—I am so glad.

Always, with much love, yours
OSCAR

[? July 1894]

MY OWN DEAR BOY—

I hope the cigarettes arrived all right—I lunched with Gladys de Grey—Reggie and Aleck Yorke there. They want me to go to Paris with them on Thursday—they say one wears flannels and straw hats and dines in the Bois—but, of course, I have no money, as usual, and can't go—Besides I want to see *you*—It is really absurd—*I can't live without you*—You are so dear, so wonderful—I think of you all day long—and miss your grace, your boyish beauty, the bright sword-play of your wit, the delicate face of your genius, so surprising always in its sudden swallow-flights towards north or south, towards sun or moon—and, above all, you yourself. The only thing consoles me is what the Sybil of Mortimer Street (whom mortals term Mrs. Robinson—) said to me—if I could disbelieve her I would—but I can't—and I know that early in January you and I will go away together for a long voyage—and that your lovely life goes always hand in hand with mine—my dear wonderful boy, I hope you are brilliant and happy. I went to Bertie today I wrote at home—then went and sat with my mother—Death and Love seem to walk on either hand as I go through life—They are the only things I think of—their winds shadow me.

London is a desert without your dainty feet, and all the buttonholes have turned to weeds—nettles and hemlock and 'the only wear'—Write me a line, and take all my love—now and for ever.

Always, and with devotion,—but I have no words for how I love you—

OSCAR

Cஒ

[July-August 1894]

DEAREST BOY—

I hope to send you the cigarettes—if Simmonds will let me have them—

He has applied for his bill—I am overdrawn £41 at the Bank—it really is intolerable the want of money—I have not a penny—I can't stand it any longer—but don't know what to do—I go down to Worthing tomorrow—I hope to do work there. The house, I hear, is very small—and I have no writing room—However, anything is better than London—

Your father is on the rampage again—been to Café Royal to enquire for us—with threats etc. I think now it wd. have been better for me to have had him bound over to keep the peace—but what a scandal! Still, it is intolerable to be dogged by a maniac—

When you come to Worthing of course all things will be done for yr. honour and joy—but I fear you may find the meals etc. tedious. But you will come—won't you? at any rate for a short time—till you are bored.

Ernesto has written to me begging for money—a very nice letter—but I really have nothing, just now.

What purple valleys of despair one goes through! Fortunately there is one person in the world to love.

Evyr. OSCAR.

᠙

[August 1894]

DEAREST BOSIE

I have just come in from luncheon—A horrid ugly Swiss governess has, I find, been looking after Cyril and Vivian for a year—she is quite impossible.
Also children at meals are tedious—
Also, you, the gilt and graceful boy, wd. be bored—
Don't come here—I will come to you.

Evyr OSCAR

᠙

[13 August 1894]

The HAVEN
5 Esplanade
Worthing.

MY OWN DEAREST BOY—

How sweet of you to send me that charming poem—I can't tell you how it touches me—and it is full of that light lyrical grace that you always have—a quality that seems so easy, to those who don't understand how difficult it is to make the white feet of poetry dance lightly among flowers without crushing them—and to those "who know" is so rare and so distinguished. I have been doing nothing here but bathing and play writing—My play is really very funny—I am quite delighted with it—But it is not shaped yet. It lies in Sibylline leaves around the room—and Arthur has twice made a chaos of it by 'tidying up'—The result, however, was rather dramatic—I am inclined to think that Chaos is a stronger evidence for an Intelligent Creator than Kosmos is: the view might be expanded.

Percy left the day after you did. He spoke much of you—Alphonso is still in favor—He is my only companion—along with Steven—Alphonso always alludes to you as 'The Lord'—which however gives you I think a Biblical Hebraic dignity that gracious Greek boys should *not* have—He also says from time to time, "Percy was the Lord's favourite" which makes me think of Percy as the infant Samuel—an inaccurate reminiscence as Percy was Hellenic.

Yesterday (Sunday) Alphonso, Stephen, and I sailed to Littlehampton in the morning—bathing on the way—We took five hours in an awful gale to come back! did not reach the pier till 11 oc. at night—pitch dark all the way—and a fearful sea—I was drenched, but was Viking-like and daring. It was, however, quite a dangerous adventure—All the fishermen were waiting for us—I flew to the hotel for hot brandy and water—on landing with my companions—and found a letter for you from dear Henry, which I send you—They had forgotten to forward it—as it was past 10 oc. on a Saturday night the proprietor could not *sell* us any brandy or spirits of any kind! So he had to *give* it to us. The result was not displeasing, but what laws! An hotel proprietor is not allowed to sell 'necessary harmless' alcohol to three shipwrecked mariners—wet to the skin—because it is Sunday! Both Alphonso and Stephen are now anarchists—I need hardly say.

Your new Sibyl is really wonderful—It is most extraordinary—I must meet her—

Dear, dear boy—you are more to me than any one of them has any idea—You are the atmosphere of beauty through which I see life—you are the incarnation of all lovely things—When we are out of tune—all colour goes from things for me—but we are never really out of tune—I think of you day and night.

Write to me soon—you honey-haired boy!—I am always devotedly

Yours, OSCAR

෴

[8 September 1894]

The HAVEN
5 Esplanade
Worthing.

MY OWN DEAR BOY—

Your sweet letter arrived this morning—and this moment I have received your delightful telegram—delightful, because I love you to think of me—What do you think of three days at Dieppe? I have a sort of longing for France—and with you—-if you can manage to come—; (I could only arrange three days—as I am so busy—)

I went yesterday up to town for the afternoon—lunched with George Alexander at the Garrick—got a little money from him—and returned by the 4.30 for dinner—so I can pay my rent, and Cyril's—(little wretch and darling,) school-fees—I dare not lodge the money in the Bank, as I have overdrawn £40—but I think of hiding gold in the garden—

Could you meet met at Newhaven on the 15th?—Dieppe is very amusing and bright. Or would you come down here first—say on Thursday: and we cd. go on?

I saw Gatby, by chance, as I was driving through Pall Mall—he stopped my cab—we had a long chat: about *you*, of course. He is one of your many admirers—Last night (see other letter)—you, and I, and the mayor figured as patrons for the entertainment given by the vagabond singers of the sands—They told me that our names, which have been placarded, all over the town, excited great enthusiasm—and certainly the Hall was crammed—I was greeted with loud applause, as I entered with Cyril: Cyril was considered to be you—

Dear boy—this is a scrawl is it not? I find farcical comedies admirable for style, but fatal to handwriting—

Do write to me—and do come to France—Is Basil *here*? If so, of course, come here—with

fondest love,
Ever devotedly,
OSCAR

[5 or 6 November 1894]

16 Tite Street
S.W.

MY DEAREST BOSIE—

I suppose you won't come up now, it is so late. Perhaps I shall hear tomorrow. I can't bear your sadness and unhappiness: because I cannot cure it. But you know what a joy it will be to see you again. I have been staying at Cannizaro from Saturday to Monday: Noel Holland, one of Knutford's sons, was there: he is partner with Edward Arnold the publisher: I told him of our idea of writing a book "How to live above one's income"—for the use of the sons of the rich: he was charmed: he seems very mad, but is quite brilliant: one of Ames's with his fiancée was there also: there were many affectionate enquiries after you—Tiny was sweet as usual: Mrs. Schuster had a black eye! a fall from her donkey-chaise: She was swathed in lace, jewels, and flowers: quite extraordinary to look at.

I heard all the details of the divorce of the Scarlet Marquis the other day: quite astonishing: Arthur Pollen told me all about it: he came to tea one afternoon.

Surely your mother intends to give you a good allowance now—when she is a little better I feel certain she will: it should be about £400 or £500 a year. It is absurd you should not have an allowance suitable to your position. I think you should speak to yr. mother about it, before you come up.

On Thursday night I am going to the first night of Tree's new play: so if you are in town I suppose you will dine with Robbie: or some other friend:

I am sending you a copy of "Hafiz" the divinest of poets—I hope the honey of his verse may charm you.

London is dripping with rain: a loathsome day.

Ever, with much love,
Yours, OSCAR

[circa 9 November 1894]

AC—[Albemarle Club]

MY DEAREST BOY,

I have been very lonely without you: and worried by money matters. Today is golden enough, but rain has dripped monotonously on all other days. I went to Haddon Chamber's play: it was not bad, but oh! so badly written! The bows and salutations of the lower orders who thronged the stalls were so cold that I felt it my duty to sit in the Royal Box with Ribblesdales, the Harry Whites, and the Home Secretary: This exasperated the wretches. How strange to live in a land where the worship of beauty, and the passion of love are considered infamous—I hate England: it is only bearable to me because you are here. Last night I supped at Willis': There were respectful enquiries after 'Lord Douglas'—

Always yours
OSCAR

[17 February 1895]

DEAREST BOY—

Yes! The Scarlet Marquis made a plot to address the audience on the first night of my play!!

Algy Burke revealed it—and he was not allowed to enter.

He left a grotesque bouquet of vegetables for me! This of course makes his conduct idiotic—robs it of dignity.

He arrived with a prize-fighter!! I had all Scotland Yard—20 police—to guard the theatre. He prowled about for 3 hours—then left chattering like a monstrous ape—Percy is on our side.

I feel now that, without yr. name being mentioned, all will go well.

I had not wished you to know—Percy wired without telling me—I am greatly touched by [your] rushing over Europe—For my own part I had determined you shd. know nothing.

I will wire to Calais and Dover—and you will of course stay with me till Saturday. I then return to Tite St, I think

Ever, with love, all love in the world,

devotedly yours
OSCAR

[2 June 1897]

Hotel de la Plage
Bernaval-sur-Mer.
Dieppe

MY DEAR BOY,

If you will send me back beautiful letters, with bitter one's of your own, of course you will never remember my address—It is as above.

Of Lugne-Poë, of course, I know nothing except that he is singularly handsome, and seems to me to have the personality of a good actor, for personality does not require intellect to help it: it is a dynamic force of its own, and is often as superbly unintelligent as the great forces of nature, like the lightning that shook at sudden moments last night over the sea that slept before my window.

The production of Salomé was the thing that turned the scale in my favour, as far as my treatment in prison by the Government was concerned, and I am deeply grateful to all concerned in it. Upon the other hand I could not give my next play for nothing, as I simply do not know how I shall live after the summer is over unless I at once make money—I am in a terrible and dangerous position—for money that I had been assured was set aside for me, was not forthcoming when I wanted it. It was a horrible disappointment: for I have of course begun to live as a man of letters should live—that is with a private sitting room and books and the like. I can see no other way of living, if I am to write, though I can see many others, if I am not.

If the Lugne-Poë can give me no money, of course I shall not consider myself bound to him. But the play in question—being religious in surroundings and treatment of subject—is not a play for a run, at all. Three performances are the most I think I could expect. All I want is to have my artistic reappearance, and own rehabilitation through art, in *Paris*, not in London. It is a homage and a debt I owe to that great city of art.

If anyone else with money would take the play, and let Lugne-Poë play the part, I would be more than content. In any case I am not bound, and, what is of more import, the play is not written! I am still trying to finish my necessary correspondence, and to express suitably my deep gratitude to all who have been kind to me.

As regards 'Le Journal,' I have the chance to write for it, and will try and get it regularly—I do not like to *abonner* myself at the office as I am anxious that my address should not be known—I think I had better do it at Dieppe, from where I get the Echo de Paris?

I hear the 'Jour' has had a sort of interview—a false one—with you. This is very distressing: as much, I don't doubt, to you as me. I hope however that it is not the cause of the duel you hint at—Once you get to fight duels in France, you have to be always doing it, and it is a nuisance. I do hope that you will always shelter yourself under the accepted right of any English gentleman to decline a duel—unless of course some personal fracas or public insult takes place.

Of course you will never dream of fighting a duel for *me*: that would be awful, and create the worst and most odious impression.

Always write to me about your art and the art of others. It is better to meet on the double peak of Parnassus than elsewhere—I have read your poems with great pleasure and interest: but on the whole your best work is to me still the work you did two years and a half ago—the ballads, the bits of the play: of course your own personality has had for many reasons to express itself *directly* since then, but I hope you will go on to forms more remote from any actual events and passions—

One can really, as I say in Intentions, be far more subjective in an *objective* form than in any other way. If I were asked of myself as a dramatist, I would say that my unique position was that I had taken the Drama, the most objective form known to art, and made it as personal a mode of expression as the Lyric or the Sonnet, while enriching the characterization of the stage, and enlarging—at any rate in the case of Salomé—its artistic horizon. You have real sympathy with the Ballad. Pray again return to it. The Ballad is the true origin of the romantic Drama, and the true predecessors of Shakespeare are not the tragic writers of the Greek or Latin State, from Aeschylus to Seneca, but the ballad-writers of the Border—In such a ballad as Gilderoy one has the prefiguring note of the romance of Romeo and Juliet, different though the plots are. The *motifs*, are, and were to me, the artistic equivalent of the refrains of old ballads. All this, is to beg you to write ballads.

I do not know whether I have to thank you or More for the books from Paris—probably both. As I have divided the books, so you must divide the thanks—

I am greatly fascinated by the Napoleon of La Jeunesse. He must be most interesting. André Gide's book fails to fascinate me. The egoistic note is, of course, and has always been to me, the primal and ultimate note of modern art, but *to be an Egoist one must have an Ego*. It is not everyone who says "I, I" who can enter into the Kingdom of Art. But I love André personally very deeply, and often thought of him in prison, as I often did of dear Reggie Cholmondeley with large Faun's eyes and honey-sweet smile. Given him my fondest love.

Evyrs.
OSCAR

Kindly forward enclosed card to Reggie, with my address, tell him to keep *both* a secret.

❧

[3 June 1897]

MY DEAR BOY,

I have just received three copies of Le Jour, that I ordered from Dieppe; not knowing what day the supposed interview with you had taken place, I had ordered the numbers for Friday, Saturday, and Sunday.

The interview is quite harmless, and I am really sorry you took any notice of it. I *do* hope it is not with the low-class journalist that you are to fight; if that absurd experience is in store for you—If you ever fight in France let it be with someone who *exists*. To fight with the dead is either vulgar farce, or a revolting tragedy.

Let me know by telegram if anything has happened. The telegraph office is at Dieppe, but they send out on swift bicyles men in fantastic dresses of the middle-class age—who blow horns all the time so that the moon shall hear them.

The costume of the 'moyen-age' is lovely, but the dress of the middle-*class* age is dreadful.

Let me beg one thing of you. Please *always* let me see *anything* that appears about myself in the Paris papers—good or bad, but especially the bad. It is a matter of vital import to me to know the attitude of the community. All mystery enrages me, and when dear More wrote to say that a false interview with you of no importance had been published, I hired a voiture at once and galloped to Dieppe to try and find it—and ordered, as I have told you, three separate numbers. It wrecks my nerves to think of things appearing on me that are kept from me. If More had enclosed it in his letter, I would have been happy and satisfied. As it was, I was really unnerved. The smallest word about me tells.

If Le Journal would publish my letter to the Daily Chronicle it would be a great thing for me. I hope you have seen it.

Ernest Dowson, Conder, and Dal Young—what a name—are coming out to dine and sleep—at least I know they dine, but I believe they don't sleep.

Evyr. OSCAR

[4 June 1897] 2.30

MY DEAR BOY,

I have just got your letter, but Ernest Dowson, Dal Young, and Conder are here, so I cannot read it—except the last three lines—I love the last words of any thing: the end in art is the beginning. Don't think I don't love you. Of course I love [you] more than anyone else. But our lives are irreparably severed, as far as meeting goes. What is left to us is the knowledge that we love each other—and every day I think of you, and I know you are a poet, and that makes you doubly dear and wonderful—My friends here have been most sweet to me, and I like them all very much—Young is the best of fellows, and Ernest has a most interesting nature. He is to send me some of his work.

We all stayed up till 3 oc.—very bad for me—but it was a delightful experience—

Today is a day of sea-fog, and rain—my first. Tomorrow I go with fishers to fish—but I will write to you tonight.

Ever, dear boy, with fondest love
OSCAR

⁓

Sunday Night
6 June [1897]

MY DEAREST BOY

I must give up this *absurd* habit of writing to you every day. It comes of course from the strange new joy of talking to you daily. But next week I must make a resolution to write to you only every seven days, and then on the question of the relations of the sonnet to modern life, and the importance of your writing romantic ballads, and the strange beauty of that lovely line of Rossetti's, suppressed till lately by his brother, where he says that, "the sea ends in a sad blueness beyond rhyme." Don't you think it lovely? "In a sad *blueness* beyond thyme." Voila "L'influence du bleu dans les arts," with a vengeance!

I am so glad you went to bed at 7 oc. Modern life is terrible to vibrating delicate frames like yours—a rose-leaf in a storm of hard hail is not so fragile. With us who are modern it is the *scabbard* that wears out the sword.

Will you do this for me—get Le Courier de la Presse to procure a copy of Le Soir, the *Brussels* paper, somewhere between the 26th and the 31st of May last—which has an article on my letter to the Chronicle, a translation of it I believe, and notice—It is of vital importance for me to have it as soon as possible. My Chronicle letter is to be published as a pamphlet with a postscript—and I need the Soir. I don't want to write myself for it, for obvious reasons. Dear boy, I hope you are still sweetly asleep—you are so absurdly sweet when you are asleep. I have been to mass at 10 oc. and to Vespers at 3 oc. I was a little bored by a sermon in the morning, but Benediction was delightful. I am seated in the Choir! I suppose sinners should have the high places near Christ's altar? I know at any rate that Christ would not turn me out.

Remember, after a few days, only *one letter a week*—I *must* school myself to it.

En attendant, Yours with all love
OSCAR

Tuesday: 15th June [1897]

MY OWN DEAR BOY,

Who posts your letters? Does anyone? Or do you ever really know the day of the month? I rarely do myself, and Ernest Dowson, who is here, never.

The reason of these tedious questions is that last night on coming from Argues-la-Bataille where I had been breakfasting with Ernest, I found a letter from you dated *June 11*. (That is last *Friday*) but *posted* June 13 (last Sunday.) I have kept the envelope for you.

You ask me in it to let you come on Saturday: but dear honey-sweet boy I have already asked you to come then: so we both have the same desire, as usual.

Your name is to be Jonquil du Vallon.

Will you write *at once* to Edward Strangman, Hotel Terminus, Gare Ste Lazare, to say you would like to see him and have news of me. He is a very gentle, rather shy chap: Irish by race, Oxford by culture: a friend of Will Rothenstein and Robbie, and a good friend of mine: he has just sent me lovely books I needed: pray let him know that I was so touched and pleased by his visit.

I suppose I shall hear at length from you today: the Facteur comes at 12 oc. and leaves at once, so all I can ever write in immediate response is a green-gray postcard. Only wine will induce the Facteur to wait. Nothing else has any influence with him.

Always devotedly
Yours OSCAR

Wednesday, 16 June [1897]

MY DEAR BOY,

I am upset with the idea that you don't get my letters, or that the post goes wrong, or something. I daresay it is all absurd, but your last three letters dated the 10th, 11th, and 12th (whereas we are now at the 16th) contain no references to things I asked you, especially as regards our meeting.

I have asked you to come here on Sunday: I have a bathing costume for you, but you had better get one in Paris. Also bring me a lot of books, and cigarettes. I cannot get good cigarettes here or at Dieppe.

The weather is very hot, so you will want a straw hat and flannels. I hope you will get quietly out of Paris. On arriving at Dieppe, take a good voiture and tell him to drive to the Hôtel *Bonnet*, Berneval-sur-Mer, and go by the road by *Puys*, not the grande route which is a straight line of white dust.

If you want a café at Dieppe on arriving, go to the Café Suisse.

It takes an hour and a half to get here, so arrive if you can at Dieppe about three o'clock and be here at five o'clock.

I hope to be in my chalet by Saturday: so you will stay with me there. I have a little walled-in place in the garden of the hotel where I have *déjeuner* and *dîner*—a bosquet of trees.

On Sunday I go to Mass, in a dark blue suit.

You must not have your letters sent on under your own name. It might do me serious harm. I will suggest—for the third time—Jonquil du Vallon, but any name you like will do.

Pray do not fail to write at once on receipt of this, and be careful of the date. Your *last* letter is dated the 12th; which was last *Saturday*.

It is lovely here today, and I am going to bathe at 10.30. Yesterday I drove Ernest Dowson back to Arques. I like him immensely.

Thanks for the 'Soir': you ask me other questions in your letter that I have answered in letters of my own to you: but I don't know if they reach you. I will wait for today's Post, and write again tomorrow.

Bring also some perfume and nice things from the sellers of the dust of roses.

Also bring yourself.

Ever yours
OSCAR

Thursday, 17 June [1897] 2 o'clock p.m.

MY DEAREST BOY,

I have been obliged to ask my friends to leave me, as I am so upset and distressed in nerve by my solicitor's letter, and the apprehension of serious danger, that simply I must be alone. I find that any worry utterly destroys my health, and makes me horrid and irritable and unkind, though I hate to be so.

Of course at present it is impossible for us to meet. I have to find out what grounds my solicitor has for his sudden action, and of course if your father—or rather Q as I only know him and think of him—if Q came over and made a scene and scandal it would utterly destroy my possible future and alienate all my friends from me. I owe to my friends everything, including the clothes I wear, and I would be wretched if I did anything that would separate them from me.

So simply we must write to each other: about the things we love, about poetry and the coloured arts of our age, and that passage of ideas into images that is the intellectual history of art. I think of you always, and love you always, but chasms of moonless nights divide us. We cannot cross it without hideous and nameless peril.

Later on, when the alarm in England is over, when secrecy is possible, and silence forms part of the world's attitude, we may meet, but at present you see it is impossible. I would be harassed, agitated, nervous. It would be no joy for me to let you see me as I am now.

You must go to some place where you can play golf and get back your lily and rose. Don't, like a good boy, telegraph to me unless on a matter of vital import: the telegraph office is seven miles off, and I have to pay the *facteur*, and also reply, and yesterday with three separate *facteurs*, and three separate replies, I was *sans le sou*, and also mentally upset in nerve. Say please to Percy that I will accept a bicycle with many thanks for his kindness: I want to get it here, where there is a great champion who teaches everyone, and has English machines: it will cost £15. If Percy will send me £15 to enclosed name and address in a cheque, it will make me very happy. Send him my card.

Ever yours (rather maimed and mutilated)

OSCAR

Wednesday June 23 [1897]

MY DARLING BOY,

Thanks for your letter received this morning: my *Fête* was a huge success: 15 gamins were entertained on strawberries and cream, apricots, chocolates, cakes and sirop de grenadine—I had a huge iced cake with Jubilee de la Reine Victoria in pink sugar just rosetted with green, and a great wreath of red roses round it all. Every child was asked beforehand to choose his present: they all chose instruments of music!!!

6 accordions
5 trompettes
4 clairons—

They sang the Marseillaise and other songs, and danced a *ronde*, and also played 'God save the Queen': they said it was 'God save the Queen,' and I did not like to differ from them. They also all had flags which I gave them. They were most gay, and sweet. I gave the health of La Reine d'Angleterre, and they cried 'Vive la Reine d'Angleterre!!!!' Then I gave 'La France'—mère de tous les artistes'—and finally I gave Le Président de la République I thought I had better do so—They cried out with one accord 'Vivent le Président de la République et *Monsieur Melmoth'!!!* So I found my name coupled with that of the President—it was an amusing experience as I am hardly more than a month out of goal.

They stayed from 4.30 to 7 oc. and played games: on leaving I gave them each a basket with a jubilee cake frosted pink and inscribed, and bonbons—

They seem to have made a great demonstration in Bernaval-le-Grand, and to have gone to the House of the Mayor and cried 'Vive Monsieur Le Maire! Vive la Reine d'Angleterre! Vive Monsieur Melmoth!'—I tremble at my position—

Today I have come in with Ernest Dowson to dine with the painter Thaulow—a giant with the temperament of Corot—I sleep here and go back tomorrow.

I will write tomorrow on things.
Ever dearest boy

Your
OSCAR

[7 July 1897]

MY DARLING BOY—

I received your letters all right and have half written my answer—

I write now on nicer things: just to know how you are, and why you stay at a place that bores you—I hear from Ernest Dowson that Montigny-Sur-Loire is lovely, and full of dear brilliant artists and sweet people. Stuart Merrill lives at Marlotte—only 3 miles off—and of course is charming and sympathetic. I hate to know you are lonely, or in danger of *ennui* that enemy of modern life.

I am waiting here for a new servant—sent to me from Avesnes—I have not yet seen him, but I hope he will be nice.

He is to come here to find me. Brutes, bald and bearded, have arrived—and Ernest Dowson says he is sure my servant is among them. It is so awful, that I am going to deny I am M. Sebastian Melmouth—

Tell me about your days. Is Gaston in waiting? Are you writing anything? Whom have you met?

Tomorrow I am going to write my poem—I will send it to you.

With my love, dearest boy,

Ever your
OSCAR

Do you know Hugues Rebell? He has just sent me his book, Nichina. Also Tristan Klingson? who sends poems. His name is so lovely I fear I shall be disappointed with his work. In fact I am.

Tuesday, 7.30 [? 31 August 1897]

MY OWN DARLING BOY,

I got your telegram half an hour ago—and just send you a line to say that I feel that my only hope of again doing beautiful work in art is being with you—It was not so in old days—but now it is different, and you can really recreate in me that energy and sense of joyous power on which Art depends—Everyone is furious with me for going back to you—but they don't understand us—I feel that it is only with you that I can do anything at all—Do remake my ruined life for me—and then our friendship and love will have a different meaning to the world—

I wish that when we met at Rouen we had not parted at all—There are such wide abysses now of space and land between us—But we love each other—

Good night—dear—
Evyr
OSCAR

∞

Letter from Alfred Douglas to Oscar Wilde

[May 15th, 1895]

MY DARLING OSCAR

Have just arrived here. It seems too dreadful to be here without you, but I hope you will join me here next week. Dieppe was too awful for anything, it is the most depressing place in the world, even Petits Chevaux was not be had, as the Casino was closed. They are very nice here, and I can stay as long as I like without paying my bill which is a good thing as I am quite penniless. The proprietor is very nice and *most* sympathetic, he asked after you at once & expressed his great indignation at the treatment you had received. I shall have to send this by a cab to the Gare du Nord to catch the post as I want you to get it first post tomorrow.

I am going to see if I can find Robert Sherard tomorrow if he is in Paris.

Charlie is with me and sends you his best love.

I had a long letter from More this morning about you. Do keep up your spirits my dearest darling, I continue to think of you day & night, and I send you all my love.

I am always your own loving & devoted boy

Bosie

"I am the love that dare not speak its name" is the final line in a poem not written by the Irish writer Oscar Wilde but in 1894 by Wilde's lover Lord Alfred Douglas, also known as Bosie. Wilde's relationship with Bosie, who was sixteen years his junior, prompted the latter's father, the Marquess of Queensberry, to state that Wilde was a homosexual, which led to two trials that ultimately ended with Wilde's imprisonment and hard labor for two years, his exile in France, and, by many accounts, the premature end of his life at age forty-six. The phrase, "the love that dare not speak its name" has been associated with Wilde ever since he became a martyr for sexual freedom and gay love, a scapegoat for society, and a myth.

Wilde did not directly mention homosexuality in today's understanding anywhere in his published writings. His best known works are his masterful plays, especially the comedies spoofing England's champagne and cucumber sandwich set, *The Importance of Being Earnest*, *Lady Windermere's Fan*, *An Ideal Husband*, and *A Woman of No Importance*, the novel *The Picture of Dorian Gray*, and the poem he wrote about his imprisonment, "The Ballad of Reading Goal." He spoke about love *in general* in all of these texts rather than the type of love for which many consider him an early crusader. Love, indeed, is Wilde's central concern, from his beginning as the author of fairy tales and gothic stories to his last writings published while living in exile in Paris after serving his two-year prison term in England. Marriage comedies endeared him to the theater-going public of his time, and the question of whether marriage shelters and compromises love leads to wider questions of how love overdetermines our lives in both exhilarating and destructive ways.

While on trial, Wilde defended relationships between men from Plato to Michelangelo and Shakespeare as an "intellectual" and nobler "form of affection." He had presented love in so many ways in his writings up to that point that he perhaps hoped describing what today we would call gay relationships as a sublimated form of love would sway a jury. It did not. But Wilde's many reflections on love, gathered in this volume from his published writings and from letters written to Lord Alfred Douglas published after Wilde's death in 1900, seem even more insightful and poignant in light of that defeat. They are—even when explicitly so only in Wilde's private letters—testimonies to one man's refusal to accept society's cruelty to gay people, or to anyone whose love for another person is unconventional. In these passages we witness a man who exposed the foibles and contradictions of his society, exploited those foibles with wonderful success, and was then punishingly brought down by them.

The format of a short book matches Wilde's penchant for epigrams and pithy phrases. Yet these are not merely entertaining quips. They anchor Wilde's artistry in the immanence of life, in real experience rather than airy, abstract philosophy. He celebrates love not as a fleeting emotion to be dismissed in favor of more substantial matters, but as the wellspring of meaningful existence. These short passages are not definitive statements but invitations to read, watch, listen to, or perform Wilde's texts. They address love as the experience that takes us out of our daily selves and beckons us to be more fully alive to ourselves and others.

Countless biographers and literary scholars have tried to make sense of the many paradoxes of Wilde's life: a husband and father put in prison for homosexuality that he refused to renounce; a celebrity brought down by scandals he anticipated in plays and his novel; a self-pitying martyr for freedom who could be calculating and cruel but changed the world for many; a decent man who used wit to pierce hypocrisy but also to perpetrate it; a master of rhetoric felled by his own words; a vain seeker of fame who ends up being true to himself at enormous cost. Paradox was Wilde's crackers and pâté, and many of his proclamations on love turn common sayings inside out to great effect. The overall intention, however, is never a cheap laugh but a costly one, because when we laugh with Wilde, we also always laugh a little at our own expense. He has been dismissed as a lightweight writer by people who also disdain melodrama as lowbrow. But Wilde was also a great classicist, an inspired literary historian and critic whose analysis of Shakespeare's love sonnets remains salient, and a master letter-writer of some fifteen hundred epistles that gradually reveal—especially in the few years after his trial and imprisonment—a sincere man behind his trademark green carnation. As an Irishman he invented in his writings a world as "though from the very beginning," parts of which we still inhabit today.[1]

The power of Wilde's language rests in how he expresses startling and surprising revelations in apparently simple terms. His humor grounds us in the things that matter—though

---

1 This is Colm Tóibín's description of Irish writers W. B. Yeats, James Joyce, and Oscar Wilde in *Mad, Bad, Dangerous to Know: The Fathers of Wilde, Yeats and Joyce* (New York: Scribner, 2018), 15.

occasionally Wilde is so enamored of his brilliance that he seems without center or purpose, as if nothing is stable for him. He makes a meal of the vagaries of daily, ordinary life, but then declares that love (once the perennial preoccupation of money has been settled) displaces most other concerns. Power, influence, status, wealth, prestige, respect: all of these play decisive roles in shaping how much actual freedom we have in making decisions about our lives. But love, in Wilde's view and in his life, can eclipse all of them in a flash. It can bring down empires and create dynasties. It destabilizes us, revealing that we may not be as securely in the world or our minds as we had thought. It brought Wilde down, who wrote on the eve of his sentencing to Alfred Douglas: "Our love has always been beautiful and noble, and if I am the butt of a terrible tragedy, it is because the nature of that love has not been understood."[2] Even when our love is understood and accepted, meaning not censured, savaged, or ridiculed, love remains an experience that lets us live life more fully in ways we cannot quite understand ourselves.

The clever ending of Wilde's *Lady Windermere's Fan* brings me to tears each time I re-read it, because there Wilde shows that even in our post-sacred age when morality is no longer based on religious authority we make choices that can devastate or redeem us. The form he chooses is melodrama, a genre easily derided and mocked by serious critics and artists for its excess and exaggerations. But what is love, for us moderns living in a disenchanted world, but the greatest vehicle for feeling something larger than life? What is love, different expressions of which dramatically clash in *Lady Windemere's Fan*, but a heightened form

---

2 April 29, 1895, letter to Lord Alfred Douglas, in: *The Complete Letters of Oscar Wilde*, eds. Merlin Holland and Rupert Hart-Davis (London: Fourth Estate, 2000), 646.

of being? Wilde's plays do not reduce you to tears or laughter with their unrivaled witticism, unexpected depth in characters who pride themselves on being superficial, and stagey plots that mirror, rather than distort, the way we act out our feelings when true love is at stake. No, when Wilde talks of love in his plays, he elevates us to tears and laughter because despite being a great ironist, he takes love so very seriously.

Wilde frequently pivots common expressions so ingrained in our thinking that it takes a rhetorical yank to show how they have curdled into cliché. He flips common phrases, often with the provocative claim that surfaces matter more than depth and that manners ought to precede morals. We learn from Wilde that our ordinary existence, when seen in the right light and from the right angle, has potential for depth and greatness, but that this potential is often buried by conventional morality and platitudes. In the plays and many of the quotations gathered here, the ordinary setting of daily life may harbor the potential for great significance, rather than the political, ideological, or religious beyond. Love, in Wilde, is unmovably *in* the world and nonetheless affords us the opportunity to leave our worlds while, strangely and wondrously, staying in it. If you've been in love, and Wilde recommends that one should be in love as many times in one's life as is feasible, you know how it can lift you out of the prosaic drone of daily life, the sameness of existence. When in love, you feel that you and the beloved truly matter. You may behave recklessly, you may recoil from the experience because it threatens to upend your world, you may throw yourself into it with complete abandon: love is the mode of being in which you surpass yourself.

But should we believe Wilde's radically secular gospel of love? "How clever you are—you never mean a thing you say.— Thank you!" is the response to this peculiar compliment in his 1893 play, *A Woman of No Importance*. Isn't Wilde warning us not to take him at his word? Isn't love a delusion, where we fool ourselves and the beloved by our mutual wish to be deceived, and the simultaneous wish to overlook the deception? Doesn't Wilde's wisdom hover over an abyss, like love songs by generic pop sirens who preach sincerity and authenticity? I wager that Wilde truly believes in love, but that he reaches this belief not intuitively, intrinsically, but by experience and reflection both. He was in love many times in his life, as many biographers have chronicled, and he turned love into the subject of many of his writings.[3] As one of the great modernists, he subjects his experience to self-analysis. Instead of deconstructing his experience into desiccated theory, however, he puts it on stage, polishes his insights to a high gloss, and reveres what in our post-sacred age we all too often dismiss. Wilde, alongside contemporaries who are radically different in temperament but similarly committed to the individual such as Henry David Thoreau, diagnosed that what we value in our age is what is statistically significant, what can be counted, what has a price. But in an era of hyperdata, what truly matters? How should we value love, as it is so often bound up with money, respect,

3   Richard Ellman's biography, *Oscar Wilde* (New York: Vintage, 1988), centers on Wilde's status as a writer while Matthew Sturgis's *Oscar: A Life* (London: Head of Zeus, 2018) draws on additional material to produce a fuller account. Nicholas Frankel's important *Oscar Wilde: The Unrepentant Years* (Cambridge, MA: Harvard University Press, 2017) shows that Wilde's life after prison was not entirely ruined but also productive, and Michele Mendelssohn's *Making Oscar Wilde* (New York: Oxford University Press, 2018) shows how Wilde turned himself into a celebrity during his 1882 U.S. lecture tour, and then into a myth. Merlin Holland and Rupert Hart-Davis's edition of *The Complete Letters of Oscar Wilde* (op. cit.) is indispensable for an understanding of Wilde's life and writings.

calculation, and exchange, but in the best of circumstances experienced as the blissfully unencumbered, innocent, incalculable meetings of two free souls?

In *Lady Windermere's Fan*, one of Wilde's dramatic alter egos states that "the cynic knows the price of everything and the value of nothing." The instant retort: "And a sentimentalist [...] is a man who sees an absurd value in everything and doesn't know the market value of any single thing." Wilde surely knows both; he is cynic and sentimentalist at once. Like Andy Warhol and Pedro Almodóvar, two of Wilde's artistic heirs who also mine the melodramatic and camp idiom of celebrity and pop culture and become celebrities themselves, he knows the market value of fine tailored clothing, real estate, and legal fees and yet sees an absurd value in love.

For Wilde, what matters is what and who is beautiful, charming, and in the best of circumstances utterly useless in his or her pursuits. He provocatively overemphasizes this dimension of life (he famously said, before dying, that either the wallpaper or he had to go) to expose the emptiness of a society that defends its morality in order to have rules to live by, instead of defending lives that are creative, imaginative, and expressive in ways that adhere to a less prescribed set of rules.

He focused on dimensions of life that are often overlooked (or distained as the business of women) and used overstatement to clarify what is really going on. The tricky thing about Wilde, like all great ironists, is that he uses irony and wit to get at what is deadly serious. Irony keeps him from seeming pedantic, plodding, lifeless, or—worst of all—sincere. Irony distances him from love, which, notwithstanding his chiding of it, cost him his career, social standing, family, income, and, in a way, ultimately his life. Wilde's wit, far from putting down or ridiculing the love he talks about, creates the distance we need to see what matters most.

Come along with Wilde to the edge of life, and tumble from there more fully into it.

NEW YORK, MARCH 2020

Oscar Wilde

Oscar Wilde was born in Dublin, Ireland, on 16 October 1854 to Sir William Wilde and his wife Jane. Wilde's mother was a successful poet and journalist who published patriotic Irish verse under the pseudonym "Speranza" and his father was a well-known surgeon, philanthropist and writer. Wilde was educated at Portora Royal School, Trinity College, Dublin, and Magdalen College at Oxford University. While at Oxford, he won literary awards, edited a literary review, and identified with the aesthetic movement that advocated "art for art's sake." After graduation, Wilde moved to London in 1879 to embark on a literary career. In 1881, he published his first book of poetry and worked as an art reviewer. In 1882 a promoter paid him to visit the United States and Canada on a far-ranging lecture tour where he entertained large crowds as the witty creator of bon mots and provocative phrases. In 1884, Wilde married Constance Lloyd, and they had two sons, Cyril and Vyvyan. To support his family, Wilde worked as editor of *Woman's World* magazine from 1887-1889.

In 1888, Wilde published *The Happy Prince and Other Tales*, fairy-stories originally invented for his two sons that touch on topics he would later address in his plays. His only novel, *The Picture of Dorian Gray* (1891), about a man who trades eternal youth by letting a painted portrait take on the signs of his sins, received largely negative reviews by Victorian critics who objected to the book's homoerotic overtones. In 1891, Wilde met Lord Alfred Douglas, nicknamed Bosie, who became his lover and whose father provoked Wilde to start the lawsuits that would ruin him. Wilde's marriage ended in 1893.

Wilde's play *Lady Windermere's Fan* opened to great success in February 1892. Very popular comedies of manners for which Wilde is still known today followed: *A Woman of No Importance* (1893), *An Ideal Husband* (1895), and *The Importance of Being Earnest* (1895).

In April 1895, Wilde sued Douglas's father for libel when the Marquess of Queensberry accused him of homosexuality. When the prosecutor furnished evidence of gay prostitutes with whom Wilde had had relations, he lost the libel case. Instead of fleeing to France immediately after the verdict, Wilde remained in London and was arrested and tried by the Crown for "gross indecency." After two trials that riveted the public and during which most of Wilde's friends, admirers, and supporters turned on him, he was sentenced to two years of hard labor. His divorced wife and sons changed their name and left England for good. While in prison Wilde wrote *De Profundis*, a dramatic monologue addressed to Bosie and later published in segments that partly disavowed their relationship.

After his release from prison in 1897, Wilde published *The Ballad of Reading Goal* to challenge inhumane prison conditions he had witnessed and suffered. In exile in France, he tried to restart his publishing career, supported by a few loyal friends but subjected to social ostracism and perpetually at the brink of financial ruin. When he reconnected with Bosie he lost most of his meager income and the support of some of the remaining friends. Unwilling to disavow Bosie, to stop associating with younger men, and to apologize to the society which had first fêted and then felled him, he died, penniless, of cerebral meningitis on November 30, 1900, in a cheap Paris hotel. Only a handful of loyal friends attended his funeral. Today his grave at Père Lachaise cemetery in Paris, where his remains were moved in 1909 by loyal supporters, is a site of pilgrimage for free spirits. The last century produced a radical reassessment of Wilde from disgraced pervert and lightweight wit to one of the most celebrated writers in English literature.

SOURCES

Oscar Wilde's works are available in many editions, including *The Complete Works of Oscar Wilde* (London: Collins, 2003), with an introduction by Merlin Holland. *Wilde on Love* is based on the following texts by Wilde.

The Happy Prince and Other Tales (1888): 28, 29, 30, 31, 32

"The Portrait of Mister W.H." (1889): 78

The Picture of Dorian Gray (1891): 5, 6, 10, 17, 18, 19, 37, 38, 39, 40, 41, 42, 43, 44, 45, 46, 47, 48, 49, 50, 51, 52, 53, 54, 55, 56, 73, 74, 75

Lady Windermere's Fan (1892): 11, 25, 26, 27, 76

A Woman of No Importance (1893): 57, 58, 59, 60, 61, 64, 65, 66, 67, 68, 69, 70, 71

The Importance of Being Earnest (1895): 7, 8, 12, 13, 14

An Ideal Husband (1895): 3, 4, 9, 16, 20, 21, 22, 23, 24, 72

"The Ballad of Reading Gaol" (1898): 77

"De Profundis" (first published 1905): 33, 34, 26

Contemplations
Great Minds on What Matters

Current and forthcoming titles in the
Warbler Press Contemplations series at
warblerpress.com